SPR
CM

The All-Together Painting

D0347706

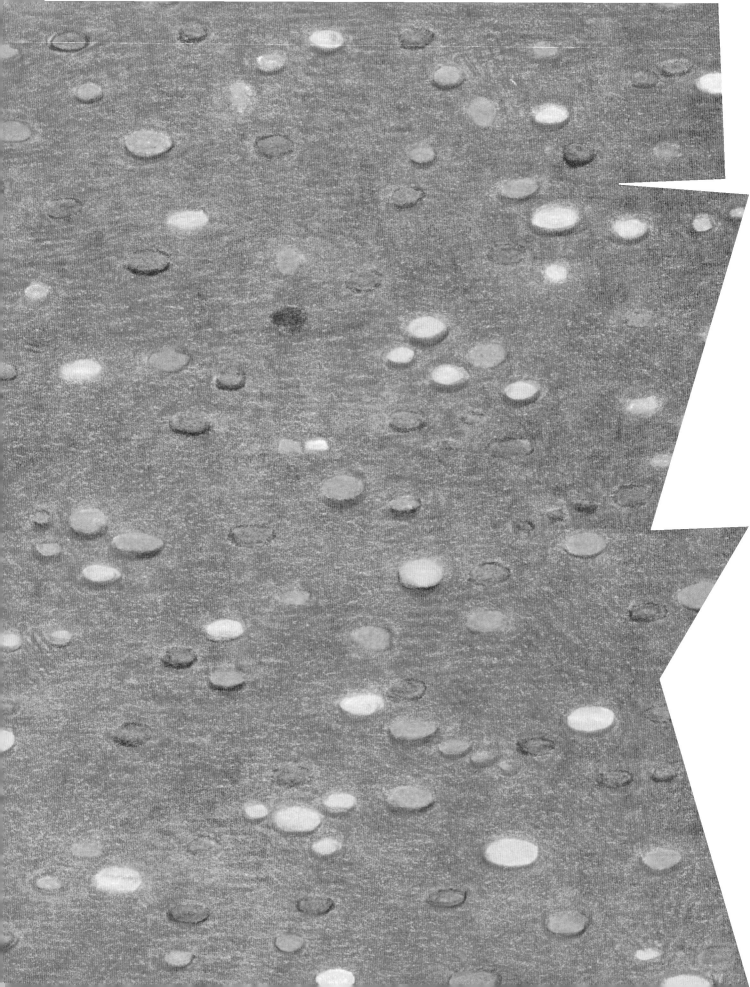

The All-Together
Painting

SCRIBBLERS

OLD Bear had been busy all afternoon painting
a picture.
'I found this tiny frame,' he told the
other toys. 'My painting of Little
Bear will just fit in nicely.'

'I WANT to paint a picture too,' said Little Bear. 'Are there any more frames?'

'There's a big one,' said Old Bear. 'Why don't you all paint a picture together? That would be fun.'

'I WANT to do my *own* painting,' said Little Bear,
'all by myself.'

'So do I,' said Rabbit.

'And me,' barked Ruff.

'OLD Bear could choose one to go in the big frame,' said Jolly Tall.

'But what shall we paint?' asked Duck. 'We can't *all* do pictures of Little Bear.'

'I don't see why not,' said Little Bear.

'I THINK I'll paint a ball,' said Ruff, 'or a spaceship or maybe a house...'

'Or just a pattern,' suggested Little Bear.

'Why don't we all do patterns?' said Rabbit. 'I think I'll paint stripes.'

HE dipped two brushes in the paint and bounced along the paper, painting lines as he went.

'Oh dear!' he sighed when he reached the end. 'My stripes are all wavy.'

'THAT'S because you bounce ^{up} and _{down,} ^{up} and _{down,} when you run,' laughed Bramwell Brown.

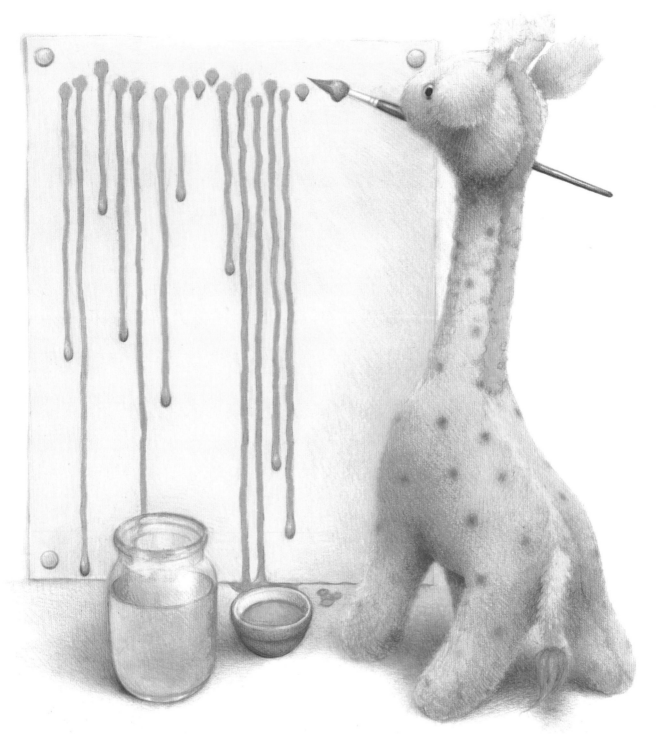

M EANWHILE Jolly had painted a row of
orange dots.

'This is my spotty pattern,' he said proudly.

BUT the paint was much too runny. The toys watched as it dribbled all the way down to the bottom of the paper.

'Your spots have turned into stripes,' said Duck.

'And they're straighter stripes than mine,' said Rabbit.

LITTLE Bear was waving his paintbrush above his head.

'Look,' he cried, 'I can make hundreds of spots. My paper is covered in them.'

'And so are you,' laughed the other toys.

'I'M doing GIANT spots,' barked Ruff. He bounced his rubber ball into the paint pot, then onto the paper.

SPLODGE!

It made a big splattered blob of yellow.

'THAT'S fun,' cried Little Bear. 'Do it again!'
But this time the ball missed the paper and landed SPLASH!
in the water.

'OH, Ruff,' cried Duck, 'now there are puddles all over my painting.'

'Sorry,' said Ruff, dabbing the splashes with a cloth. 'Is that better?'

'It isn't quite the pattern I wanted,' grumbled Duck.

'I T'S lovely!' said Old Bear, as
he arrived to collect the paintings.
'In fact, all your patterns are
perfect.'

'*I* don't think so,' said Duck,
staring at the dribbles and
splodges and wiggly lines.

'Just wait and see,' called
Old Bear, as he hurried
away.

THE toys were still clearing away the painting things when Old Bear returned a little later.

'Now cover your eyes and come with me,' he said, 'and no peeping till we're there!'

OLD Bear led the toys to a large picture propped against the wall. 'Now you can look,' he said.

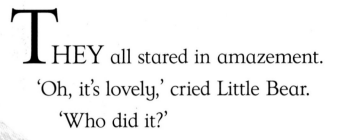

THEY all stared in amazement.
'Oh, it's lovely,' cried Little Bear.
'Who did it?'

'YOU all did,' laughed Old Bear. 'I just cut out your patterns and stuck them together. Look, Jolly's orange stripes are the boat and Rabbit's wavy lines are the sea.'

'So Ruff's yellow splodge is the sun,' said Duck, 'and I must have painted the sky.'

'I CAN see my spots,' cried Little Bear, 'on the sails of the boat.'

'That's right,' said Old Bear, 'and you all did the patterns on the fish.'

'So we did an all-together painting after all,' laughed Little Bear, 'and it was fun!'

'I said it would be,' laughed Old Bear.

'A ND now, after all our hard work, let's have an all-together tea!'

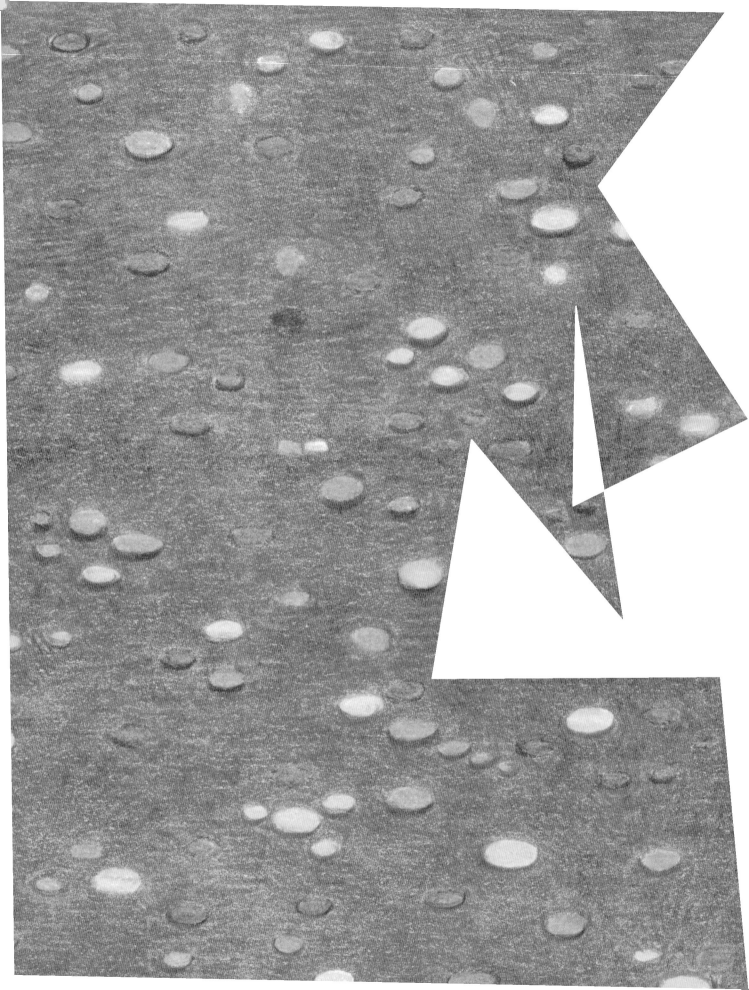

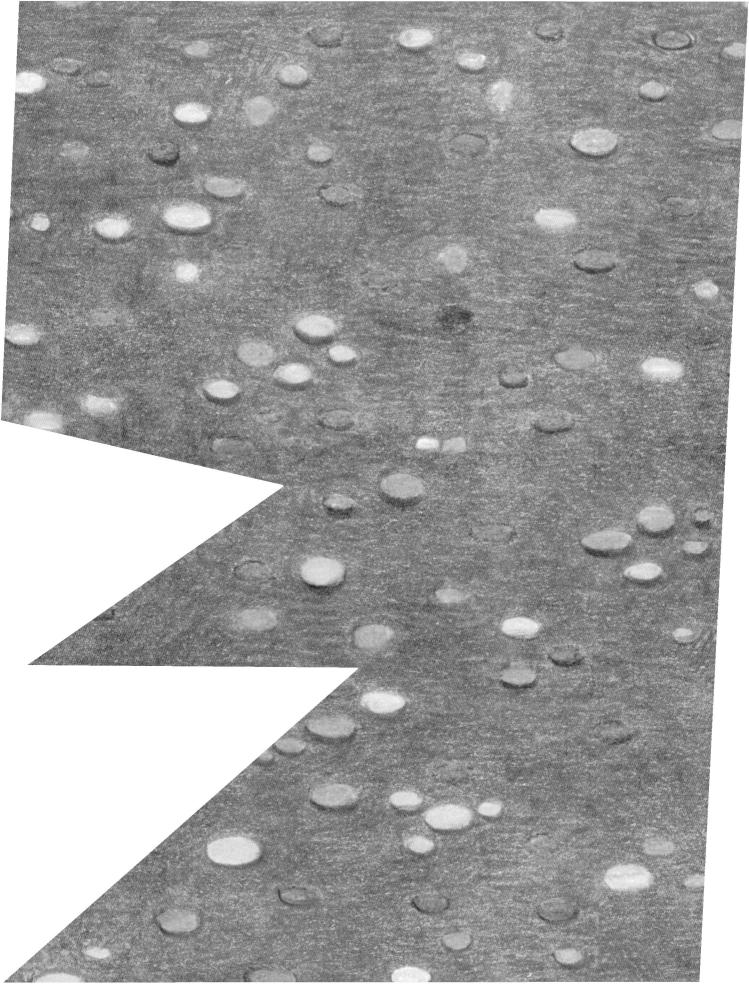

For Sharmon, Nathene and Christine

SALARIYA

www.salariya.com

This edition published in Great Britain in MMXIII by Scribblers, a division of Book House,
an imprint of The Salariya Book Company Ltd
25 Marlborough Place,
Brighton BN1 1UB

www.scribblersbooks.com
www.janehissey.co.uk

First published in Great Britain in MMI by Hutchinson Children's Books

© The Salariya Book Company Ltd MMXIII
Text and illustrations © Jane Hissey MMI, MMXIII

All rights reserved. No part of this publication may be reproduced, stored in or introduced into a retrieval system or
transmitted in any form, or by any means (electronic, mechanical, photocopying, recording or otherwise) without the
written permission of the publisher. Any person who does any unauthorised act in relation to this publication may be
liable to criminal prosecution and civil claims for damages.

ISBN-13: 978-1-908973-71-9

1 3 5 7 9 8 6 4 2

A CIP catalogue record for this book is available from the British Library.

Printed and bound in China
Printed on paper from sustainable sources

This book is sold subject to the conditions that it shall not, by way of trade or otherwise, be lent, resold, hired out, or
otherwise circulated without the publisher's prior consent in any form or binding or cover other than that in which it is
published and without similar condition being imposed on the subsequent purchaser.